PUFFIN BOOKS

Dumpling

Dumpling

Dick King-Smith

Illustrated by
Jo Davies

PUFFIN BOOKS

PUFFIN BOOKS

Published by the Penguin Group
Penguin Books Ltd, 27 Wrights Lane, London W8 5TZ, England
Penguin Putnam Inc., 375 Hudson Street, New York, New York 10014, USA
Penguin Books Australia Ltd, Ringwood, Victoria, Australia
Penguin Books Canada Ltd, 10 Alcorn Avenue, Toronto, Ontario, Canada M4V 3B2
Penguin Books (NZ) Ltd, Private Bag 102902, NSMC, Auckland, New Zealand

Penguin Books Ltd, Registered Offices: Harmondsworth, Middlesex, England

First published by Hamish Hamilton Ltd 1986
Published in Puffin Books 1995
13 15 17 19 20 18 16 14 12

Text copyright © Fox Busters Ltd, 1986
Illustrations copyright © Jo Davies, 1986
All rights reserved

The moral right of the author and illustrator has been asserted

Printed in Hong Kong by Midas Printing Limited

"Oh, how I long to be long!" said Dumpling.

"Who do you want to belong to?" asked one of her brothers.

"No, I don't mean *to belong*," said Dumpling. "I mean, to BE LONG!"

5

When the three dachshund puppies had
been born, they had looked much like
pups of any other breed.

Then, as they became older, the two brothers began to grow long, as dachshunds do. Their noses moved further and further away from their tail-tips.

But the third puppy stayed short and stumpy.

"How *long* you are getting," said the lady who owned them all to the two brothers.

She called one of them Joker because he was always playing silly games, and the other one Thinker, because he liked to sit and think deeply.

Then she looked at their sister and shook her head.

"You are nice and healthy," she said. "Your eyes are bright and your coat is shining and you're good and plump. But dachshunds are supposed to have long bodies, you know. And you haven't. You're just a little dumpling."

Dumpling asked her mother about the problem.

"Will I ever grow really long like Joker and Thinker?" she asked.

Her mother looked at her plump daughter and sighed.

"Time will tell," she said.

Dumpling asked her brother, Joker.

"Joker," she said. "How can I grow longer?"

"That's easy, Dumpy," said Joker. "I'll hold your nose and Thinker will hold your tail and we'll stretch you."

"Don't be silly, Joker," said Thinker.
Thinker was a serious puppy. He did
not like to play jokes. "It would hurt
Dumpy if we did that."

"Well then, what shall I do, Thinker?"
asked Dumpling.

Thinker thought deeply. Then he said,
"Try going for long walks. And it helps if
you take very long steps."

So Dumpling set off the next morning.
All the dachshunds were out in the
garden. The puppies' mother was
snoozing in the sunshine.

Joker was playing a silly game
pretending that a stick was a snake.

Thinker was sitting and thinking
deeply.

Dumpling slipped away through a hole in the hedge.

Next to the garden was a wood, and she
set off between the trees on her very short
legs. She stepped out boldly, trying hard
to imagine herself growing a tiny bit
longer with each step.

Suddenly she bumped into a large
black cat which was sitting under a yew
tree.

"Oh, I beg your pardon!" said
Dumpling.

"Granted," said the cat. "Where are
you going?"

"Oh, nowhere special. I'm just taking a
long walk. You see, I'm trying to grow
longer," and she went on to explain about
dachshunds and how they should look.

"Everyone calls me Dumpling," she said sadly. "I wish I could be long."

"Granted," said the black cat again.

"What do you mean," she said. "Can you make me long?"

"Easy as winking," said the cat, winking.

"I'm a witch's cat. I'll cast a spell on you. How long do you want to be?"

"Oh very, very long!" cried Dumpling excitedly. "The longest dachshund ever!"

The black cat stared at her with his green eyes, and then he shut them and began to chant:

"Abra-cat-abra,
Hark to my song,
It will make you
Very long."

The sound of the cat's voice died away and the wood was suddenly very still.

Then the cat gave himself a shake and opened his eyes.

"Remember," he said, "you asked for it."

"Oh, thank you, thank you!" said Dumpling. "I feel longer already. Will I see you again?"

"I shouldn't wonder," said the cat.

Dumpling set off back towards the garden. The feeling of growing longer was lovely. She wagged her tail madly, and each wag seemed a little further away than the last.

She thought how surprised Joker and Thinker would be. She would be much longer than them.

"Dumpling, indeed!" she said. "I will have to have a new name now, a very long one to match my new body."

But then she began to find walking
difficult. Her front feet knew where they
were going, but her back feet acted very
oddly. They seemed to be a long way
behind her.

They kept tripping over things,
and dropping into rabbit-holes.

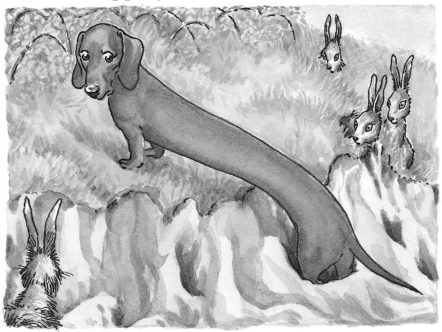

They kept getting stuck among the bushes. She couldn't see her tail, so she went round a big tree to look for it and met it on the other side.

By now, she was wriggling on her tummy like a snake.

"Help!" yapped Dumpling at the top of her voice. "Cat, come back, please!"

"Granted," said the witch's cat, appearing suddenly beside her. "What's the trouble now?"

"Oh please," cried Dumpling, "undo your spell!"

"Some people are never satisfied," said the cat. Once more he stared at her with his green eyes.

Then he shut them and began to chant:

"Abra-cat-abra,
Hear my song,
It will make you
Short not long."

Dumpling never forgot how wonderful it felt as her back feet came towards her front ones, and her tummy rose from the ground.

She hurried homewards, and squeezed her nice, comfortable, short, stumpy body through the hole in the hedge.

Joker and Thinker came galloping
across the grass towards her.

How clumsy they look, she thought,
with those silly long bodies.

"Where have you been, Dumpy?"
shouted Joker.

"Did the exercise make you longer?"
asked Thinker.

"No," said Dumpling. "But as a matter of fact, I'm quite happy as I am now.

"And that's about the long and the short of it!"